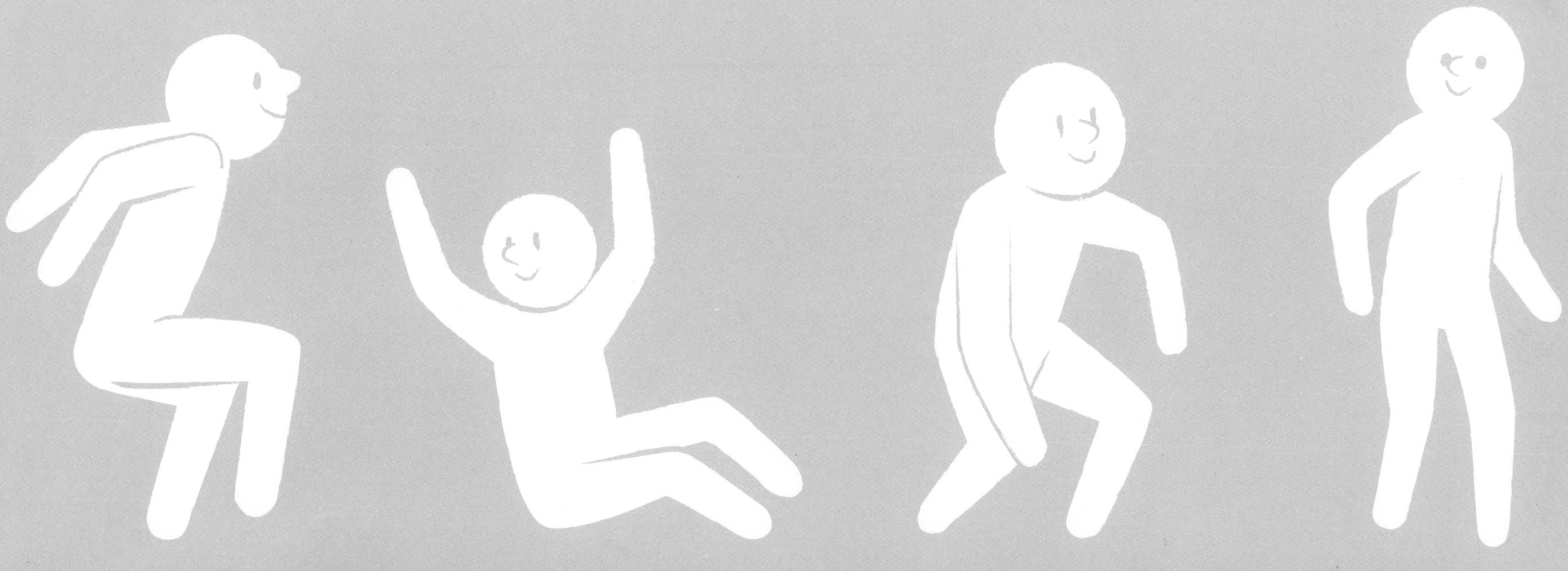

BROADWAY

Mr. Walker Steps Out

WITHDRAWN

by Lisa Graff

Illustrated by Christophe Jacques

Clarion Books | Houghton Mifflin Harcourt | Boston New York

CLARION BOOKS
3 Park Avenue
New York, New York 10016

Clarion Books is an imprint of
Houghton Mifflin Harcourt Publishing Company.

hmhbooks.com

The illustrations in this book were done digitally.
The text was set in Rotis Sans Serif Std.
Cover design by Sharismar Rodriguez and Kaitlin Yang
Interior design by Sharismar Rodriguez

Library of Congress Cataloging-in-Publication Data
is available.

ISBN 978-1-328-85103-1

Manufactured in China
SCP 10 9 8 7 6 5 4 3 2 1
4500823883

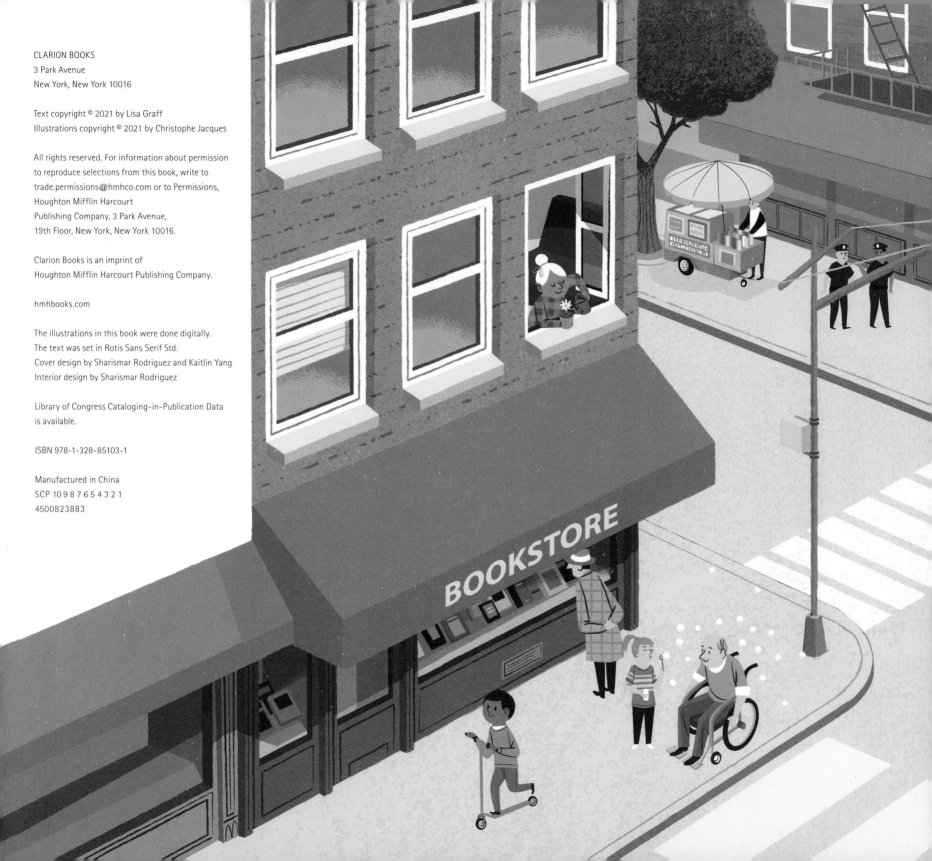

To Owen —**L.G.**

For Vero, Pieter, Dave, and Christy,
for all their help and support —**C.J.**

Mr. Walker worked very hard.

Every day, he stood in the window of his boxy little house on the corner of Broadway and Main and let people know when it was safe to cross the street.

When it was not safe, he held up a big red hand
so everyone would stop and wait.

As he worked, Mr. Walker watched lots of wonderful things happening just beyond his window. He saw puddles being splashed and bikes being ridden, kids licking towers of ice cream, and dogs tugging owners on their leashes.

Most days, watching was more than enough.

But sometimes, Mr. Walker wished he could step out of his boxy little house and do something wonderful himself.

So, one day, he did.

Mr. Walker propped up the big red hand in the window of
his boxy little house and jumped down to the sidewalk below.

Leaving was easy.
He wondered why he'd never done it before.

When it was safe to cross the street, Mr. Walker crossed.

And right away, he started doing wonderful things.

With each new thing he tried, Mr. Walker felt just a little bit bigger than he'd been the day before.

It was a very nice feeling.

So Mr. Walker hopped on a bus downtown, where he could do even more wonderful things. Things he had never dreamed of doing.

Some things were silly.

Some were strange.

Some were scary.

Some were downright magical.

With each day that passed, Mr. Walker found more wonderful things to do.

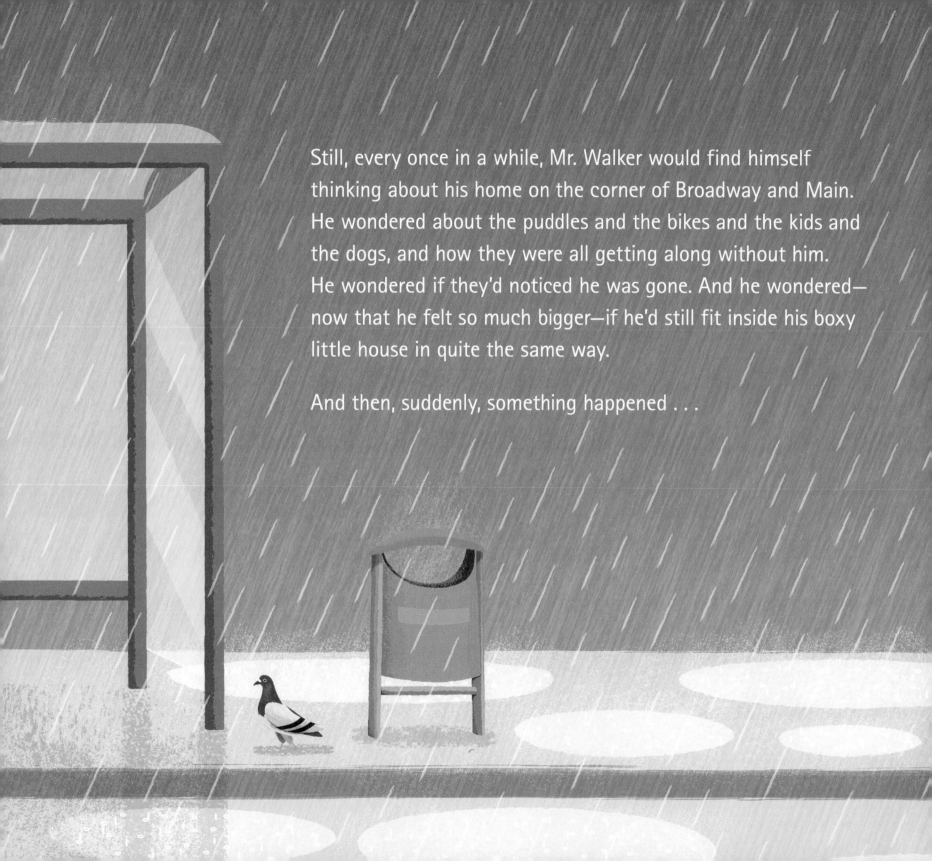

Still, every once in a while, Mr. Walker would find himself
thinking about his home on the corner of Broadway and Main.
He wondered about the puddles and the bikes and the kids and
the dogs, and how they were all getting along without him.
He wondered if they'd noticed he was gone. And he wondered—
now that he felt so much bigger—if he'd still fit inside his boxy
little house in quite the same way.

And then, suddenly, something happened . . .

. . . something very, *very* big.

On the street in front of him, a truck's tires screeched.

Horns honked. Cars swerved. Dogs barked. People shouted.

FINE ARTS

And in the middle of it all, someone stood frozen—
someone very, very small. It was a little girl,
Mr. Walker saw, who was trying to cross the street.

Without thinking about whether he was doing something big
or something small, Mr. Walker took the little girl's hand.

And, when it was safe to go, he helped her cross the street.

That afternoon, Mr. Walker made his way back to the corner of Broadway and Main.
He found that he'd missed his corner quite a bit.

As it turned out, his corner had missed him too.

When Mr. Walker climbed back into his boxy house, it didn't feel nearly as small as it had before. It seemed to have grown while he was gone, just the same as he had.

Mr. Walker fit perfectly.

He took down the red hand that he'd propped up in the window. And he signaled to the people that it was safe to cross the street.

From that day on, whenever Mr. Walker watched the big, wonderful world from the window of his not-so-little house, he felt proud. Because he knew that he was an important part of it all.

But even the most important people need vacations sometimes.

31901066819980